FLORA'S FANTASTIC REVENGE

Nick Warburton was a primary school teacher for ten years before deciding to become a full-time writer. He has written plays for stage, television and radio, including *Conversations from the Engine Room*, which won the 1985 Radio Times Drama Award. He has also written a number of children's books, among them *The Battle of Baked Bean Alley*, *Normal Nesbitt*, *Dennis Dipp on Gilbert's Pond* and *Lost In Africa*. A Visiting Fellow of Chichester University, Nick is married with a son and lives in Cambridge.

Books by the same author
for older readers

Dennis Dipp on Gilbert's Pond
Gladiators Never Blink

NICK WARBURTON

Illustrations by Cathy Gale

WALKER BOOKS
AND SUBSIDIARIES
LONDON • BOSTON • SYDNEY

For Freddie

First published 2000 by
Walker Books Ltd, 87 Vauxhall Walk
London SE11 5HJ

This edition published 2001

2 4 6 8 10 9 7 5 3 1

Text © 2000 Nick Warburton
Illustrations © 2000, 2001 Cathy Gale

The right of Nick Warburton to be identified as author of this
work has been asserted by him in accordance with the
Copyright, Designs and Patents Act 1988

This book has been typeset in Garamond

Printed and bound in Great Britain by The Guernsey Press Co. Ltd

British Library Cataloguing in Publication Data:
a catalogue record for this book is
available from the British Library

ISBN 0-7445-7898-1

CONTENTS

Lurking and Listening
9

Windows Big and Small
16

Splendiflora Fantastica
25

The Perfect Mixture
37

Flower Power
52

LURKING AND LISTENING

Emma and Will were watching Mr Petchy pottering about in his front garden. Mr Petchy had a very big front garden because he lived in the big house on the corner.

He was getting ready for his Flower
Show. He had a flower show every
year and invited everyone to come
and see the most amazing plants.

"The plants are so amazing because he has green fingers," Emma said.

"Green fingers?" said Will. "You mean they're not ripe?"

"No. It means he has a special way with plants, that's all."

But as Mr Petchy pottered about, Will thought there really *was* a faint green tinge to his fingers.

They watched him working away at his plants and putting up stalls for games and cakes and toffee-apples. It isn't just plants he has a special way with, thought Will.

They watched him fill his watering-can from an overgrown, dark-green pond.

Mr Petchy's Flower Show raised money for charity, so of course, Will and Emma liked to do their bit.

Last year they'd grown some seeds, but Trevor Tapp had poured something nasty in the flowerpot when they weren't looking.

Big, brawny Trevor Tapp lived over the road. He liked spoiling things. Will and Emma's plants came up weedy and floppy, and nobody bought them.

The year before that, they'd made
some buns, but Trevor Tapp had
slipped something nasty in the
mixture and the buns turned out all
wrong. The vicar bought one and
then went behind the first-aid tent
to be sick. So they didn't make
much money then, either.

They thought they'd try something different this year.

"I know," said Will. "We can clean windows for people."

But Trevor Tapp was lurking and listening. He heard every word, and sniggered and rubbed his hands.

WINDOWS BIG AND SMALL

Will and Emma went home to make a sign for their new business. They propped it by the front gate and went indoors to wait for their first customer.

They waited ... and waited.
Nobody came.

So they went back outside to see
where everyone was. Across the
road they saw a big, brawny boy
cleaning windows. It was Trevor
Tapp, busily spoiling their plans.

"Oh well," Emma said. "Maybe we can share the windows with Trevor. Pop over and speak to him about it."

"He'll turn nasty and slosh water over me," said Will. "He's that kind of boy."

"He might not."

Will sighed and crossed the road.
Trevor Tapp saw him coming and
sloshed water over him.

"Don't mind me," he laughed.
"I'm only having a bit of fun!"
Will trudged back, dripping wet.
"Now what?" he said.

"We must carry on," said Emma. "*Someone* will see our sign soon."

"Let's move it to a better place," said Will.

But when they moved the sign, they saw exactly what was wrong. Someone had added two new words.

Windows cleaned by Will and Emma. **NOT** very cheap. **NOT** For charity.

They were changing the words
back again when Mr Petchy himself
came by and stopped to look.

"Do you do *big* windows, or
small windows?" he asked.

"Then here's two small windows for you." He took his glasses off and handed them to Emma.

A pair of glasses! That wasn't much of a job. All the same, Will dipped the glasses in a bucket and Emma rubbed them with a cloth. They came up sparkling.

"Good," said Mr Petchy.

"That's two pence for each
window. Four pence altogether."
    Then they heard a horrible
hooting sound from over the road.
It was Trevor Tapp, laughing.

"Take no notice," Mr Petchy told them. "You did a good job so now you can clean some *big* windows. Come with me and I'll show you."

SPLENDIFLORA FANTASTICA

Mr Petchy marched them to a heavy door at the side of his house and took a large key from his pocket.

Will and Emma held their breath. Mr Petchy was going to take them into the back garden, a place where no one ever went!

The door creaked open. There in the distance were the windows Mr Petchy wanted them to clean. The biggest greenhouse they'd ever seen!

"There must be lots of plants in that," said Will.

"Come and see," Mr Petchy said. "Come and meet Flora."

He opened the greenhouse door but they could see no sign of Flora. All they saw was one huge flower pot with a single plant in it. A spindly, thin plant with a floppy stem and one weedy leaf.

"We had some like that," Emma said.

"Not like this. This is the Splendiflora Fantastica. The only one in the country," said Mr Petchy.

It didn't look like a Splendiflora Fantastica. It looked like a soggy drinking straw.

"Where's Flora?" Emma asked, looking round.

"This is Flora," said Mr Petchy and he pointed at the plant. "She won't flower, though. I've tried everything."

He waved his fingers at the plant. They *are* green, thought Will. But nothing happened.

Mr Petchy went indoors and left them to get on. In no time at all they were wiping and polishing the greenhouse glass, inside and out.

After a while, Will noticed that the hedge at the bottom of the garden was moving. It jiggled and trembled.

Sure enough, a big, brawny face was poking through the leaves. Then the face disappeared.

Will and Emma went down the garden to see what Trevor Tapp was up to.

On the other side of the hedge was a field. In the field were three quiet cows chewing the grass, and Trevor Tapp running about with a bucket and spade. Backwards and forwards he went, stopping here and there to shovel something into the bucket.

"What *is* he doing?" Will said.

"Collecting cowpats, I think," said Emma.

"Don't mind me," Trevor Tapp called to them. "I'm only having a bit of fun."

When his bucket was full, he stirred the mixture with his spade. Then he carried it over to the hedge. He began to swing the bucket.

"He's going to throw it!" said Will. "Quick! Do something!"

THE PERFECT MiXTURE

"One…"

"He'll spoil all our work!" Emma yelled.

"Two…"

They ran to the greenhouse, but what *could* they do? They couldn't move it. They couldn't cover it.

"THREE!" shouted Trevor Tapp.

A sloppy brown mess came flying over the hedge like a huge, dark rain-cloud. Straight for the greenhouse. Will jumped in the way and spread his arms. It was the only thing he could think of.

There was a slurping, smacking sound and he disappeared beneath the sloppy brown mess. And there he stood – a brown snowman with blinking eyes.

Trevor Tapp stuck his face
through the hedge and hooted.
"Look at him!" he chortled. "And
look at your sparkling windows!"

Half the greenhouse was covered
with muck. There were only two
clean patches. One was shaped
like Will with his arms spread out.
The other was the open door.

"Oh no!" cried Emma. "The Splendiflora Fantastica!"

She ran in to see if it was all right and...

Disaster.

A dollop of cowpat had landed in the flower pot. Another dollop dripped from the single, weedy leaf.

"We'll just have to clear up," said Emma firmly, "and start again."

But there was no time to clear up. Mr Petchy was striding down the garden.

"What have you done to my lovely Flora?" he cried.

The garden was full of noise. Trevor Tapp laughing behind the hedge. Mr Petchy shouting. Birds screeching and cows mooing.

Then there was another sound.
A faint rustling.

"Listen," Emma said, holding up
her hand. "What's that?"

Mr Petchy stopped shouting and
listened. The birds and the cows
cocked their heads and listened, too.

The rustling was getting louder.
A thick green stem curled out of
the greenhouse. It twisted up the
side and climbed to the roof. As it
went, big leaves unfolded. Lush,
sprouting leaves as big as shirts on
a washing-line.

"It's the Splendiflora Fantastica,"
said Emma quietly. "It's growing."

More and more stems came out
of the greenhouse. One gripped a
garden fork and tossed it in the air.
Another twined round a
wheelbarrow and pushed it aside.

Along each stem were buds the
size of coconuts. One of them burst
open – POP! – and the strangest,
most dazzling flower appeared.

"Oh Flora, my beauty!" said Mr
Petchy with tears of joy in his eyes.
"You're flowering at last!"

"It's magic," Will said in a whisper.

"It's cowpats!" said Emma.

"Cowpats!" cried Mr Petchy.
"I never thought of cowpats. Well done, well done!"

The birds watched with their beaks hanging open. Four astonished faces stared through the hedge – Trevor Tapp and the three cows. The cows seemed rather pleased with themselves.

POP! POP! More flowers burst open and Mr Petchy's garden was alive with colour and movement.

Then one of the stems twisted towards the hedge. It lifted itself and swayed from side to side. Trevor Tapp's head disappeared and he went running away across the field.

FLOWER POWER

People came from miles around to see the Splendiflora Fantastica at the Flower Show. There were cameras and microphones and reporters all over the place.

Everyone wanted to know about this wonderful new flower. And who was there to answer all their questions? Trevor Tapp, of course.

He stood in the middle of an excited crowd, boasting about how he had discovered the secret of the cowpats.

"It was all my doing," he said.

He didn't notice the thick green stem creeping through the crowd to curl round his ankle. He was folding his arms to pose for a picture when he felt a tug – and down he went.

"Help!"

The Splendiflora Fantastica didn't help. It dragged him backwards across the lawn.

"Ow! Urgh!
Nn-neeuugh-EECH!"
And Trevor Tapp
was dangling by his
ankle in the
air. One

moment
he was
over the cake stall...
"WH-OA!"
...and the
next he

was upside-down
above the pond.
"WHO-OAH! Help!

Help! Get me down
from here!"

It was the highlight of the show —
a boy being swung through the air
by a plant. Cameras flashed and
people *oohed* and *aahed* with
wonder.

"You'd better let go, Flora, my
sweet," Mr Petchy said to his plant.

He wagged a green finger at it –
and the Splendiflora Fantastica
let go.

Down came Trevor with a slap and a slurp. Mr Petchy's pond was a muddy one, a soup of ooze. Slimy things were in that pond, and now Trevor Tapp was in there with them.

The crowd fell silent. Then a
sludgy head bobbed to the surface,
dripping with mud. The plant
opened and shut its flowers a little,
like someone winking.

"Don't mind Flora," Emma and
Will told Trevor Tapp. "She's only
having a bit of fun!"

More  for you to enjoy!

- *Little Stupendo Flies High* Jon Blake   0-7445-5970-7

- *Captain Abdul's Pirate School* Colin McNaughton   0-7445-5242-7

- *The Ghost in Annie's Room* Philippa Pearce   0-7445-5993-6

- *Molly and the Beanstalk* Pippa Goodhart   0-7445-5981-2

- *Taking the Cat's Way Home* Jan Mark   0-7445-8268-7

- *The Finger-eater* Dick King-Smith   0-7445-8269-5

- *Care of Henry* Anne Fine   0-7445-8270-9

- *The Impossible Parents Go Green* Brian Patten   0-7445-7881-7

- *Flora's Fantastic Revenge* Nick Warburton   0-7445-7898-1

- *Jolly Roger* Colin McNaughton   0-7445-8293-8

- *The Haunting of Pip Parker* Anne Fine   0-7445-8294-6

- *Tarquin the Wonder Horse* June Crebbin   0-7445-7882-5

All at £3.99